LANA's WORLD

LET'S GO TO THE MOON!

To the newest little Levy, Rafael Tinen Levy,
and his big brother, Daniel, with love —E.S.

For my Super-Brother, Andrew —J.G.

All rights reserved. Green Light Readers and its logo are trademarks of
HMH Publishers LLC, registered in the United States and other countries.

For information about permission to reproduce selections from this book, write
to trade.permissions@hmhco.com or to Permissions, Houghton Mifflin Harcourt
Publishing Company, 3 Park Avenue, 19th Floor, New York, New York 10016.

www.hmhco.com

The text of this book is set in Caecelia LT Std.
The display type was set in Gil Sans.
The illustrations were made with watercolors, pastels, and colored pencils.

Library of Congress Cataloging-in-Publication Data is on file.

ISBN: 978-0-544-86760-4 hardcover
ISBN: 978-0-544-86761-1 paperback

Manufactured in China
SCP 10 9 8 7 6 5 4 3 2 1
4500646958

LANA's WORLD

LET'S GO TO THE MOON?

Written by **Erica Silverman**

Illustrated by **Jess Golden**

GREEN LIGHT READERS
HOUGHTON MIFFLIN HARCOURT
BOSTON NEW YORK

Mama and Papa were raking leaves.

"Let's go to the moon," said Lana.

"The moon is far away," said Mama.

"The moon is lonely," said Papa.

"There's a *man* in the moon," said Lana.

Jay and Ray were jumping
on their trampoline.

"Let's go to the moon," said Lana.

"The moon has no gravity," said Jay.

"You might float away," said Ray.

"Furry won't let me float away,"
said Lana. "Come, Furry!"

But Furry was chasing leaves.

"I will go to the moon
by myself," said Lana.

In her room, Lana took out glow-in-the-dark stickers. She stuck stars and planets everywhere.

She made a rocket out of boxes.
She put on her space suit
and climbed on board.

"Now . . . let's go to the moon,"
whispered Lana.

Her room became a launch site.
"Three . . . two . . . one . . . blastoff!"
The rocket rattled and roared.
Vroom!
Zoom!
Whoosh!

Up Lana soared!
Up through dark space.
Up past bright stars!
She landed on the moon.

Lana stepped outside
and looked around.
"Helloooo, Man in the Moon!"
she called. "Helloooo!"

Silence.

The moon *is* lonely, thought Lana.

But then . . . someone answered:

"Helloooo, Earth Girl!"

Lana saw the man in the moon!

And the woman in the moon.
"Welcome, Earth Girl," said the
moon woman.

Lana saw two moon boys.
They glided toward her.

"I'm Super-Nova,"
said one moon boy.

"I'm Ninja-Nova,"
said the other.

"Come look around," said the moon man.

"Will I float away?" asked Lana.

"Hold this rope," said the moon woman.

"Hold tight," said Super-Nova.

"Don't let go," said Ninja-Nova.

They hiked up hills.

They rolled down craters.

They kicked up puffs
of moon dust.

"Maybe . . ." said Lana, "I could
float a little."
They let out the rope.

Up and down she bounced.

"Wheeeeee!" Lana squealed.

"I love the moon!"

Suddenly, something big and hairy charged at her.

"Is that a moon m-m-monster?" asked Lana.

"He's our moon beast,"
said Super-Nova.
"He's a tame moon beast,"
said Ninja-Nova.

Lana petted the beast.

"I wish I had a treat for you," she said.

She looked around.

"I'd like a treat for me, too."

"We have moon rocks," said Super-Nova.

"Have a moon rock," said Ninja-Nova.

"No thanks," said Lana.

Her tummy rumbled.

"It's time to go home."

She climbed into her rocket.

Everyone waved goodbye.

"Three . . . two . . . one . . . blastoff!"

The rocket rattled and roared.

Vroom!

Zoom!

Whoosh!

Up Lana soared!
Up through dark space!
Up past bright stars!

She landed on Earth.

"Welcome home!" shouted Mama,
Papa, Jay, and Ray.

"Woof!" barked Furry.

"It's great to be home," said Lana.
They all baked moon cookies.

And Lana gave Furry a dog biscuit
as round as the moon.